The Unicorn Who Wore a **Tutu**

Cynthia Hickey

ISBN:978-1-959788-14-0

Dedicated to Emma, the lover of rainbows and unicorns.

In a magical kingdom in a faraway land there lived a
unicorn princess named Emma. Other than her parents,
she loved two things very much. Rainbows and dancing.

She danced everywhere she went and every chance she
got, even when she had other things she should do.

One day, Emma sat in the meadow planning some new dance moves. She studied the butterflies and the flowers wanting to sway and flutter like they did.

She was so deep into her thoughts, she forgot she was supposed to clean her room until her mother yelled out the palace window.

EMMA! Clean your room!

Her room wasn't that messy. Just a few things lying around.

What was the big deal? She would do it later. Right before dinner.

When it became time for supper, Emma meant to head home and clean her room. Really, she did.

But the butterflies invited her to dance with them.

"Follow us," they said. "We know some magical places to dance in."

She thought about it for a moment, and looked back at the castle. Would she be back before her mother got mad?

The thrill of a dancing adventure tugged at her. She galloped after the butterflies.

She danced among giant mushrooms. She had so much fun, she didn't hear the butterflies tell her they had to go home to eat. Emma kept dancing.

When she danced across a waterfall, she should've looked up at the rainbow. Emma was no longer alone.

She started to think she might be lost.

Emma liked dancing and rainbows, but she did not like being lost and alone. This made her very sad.

On her first night alone, it started to rain. Emma only liked the rain when she was warm and snug in her room.

Emma dreamed all night about her messy room and wished very much that she had listened to her mother and cleaned it. If she had listened and not followed the butterflies, she wouldn't be lost in the dark and rain.

When the rain continued and Emma noticed the witch in the sky, she decided it was time to keep going. She'd never find her way home by hiding under a tree.

Her travels took her through some magical landscapes full of color and strange flowers.

But everywhere Emma went, the witch followed.

When Emma finally called out to ask the witch what she wanted, the scary woman simply waved for her to follow.

After thinking for a good long minute, Emma decided to follow. Maybe the witch could help her instead of hurt her.

"How much farther," Emma asked.
The witch only smiled and waved.

Strange landscape after strange landscape led to another nightfall. Still the witch flew on, luring Emma after her. Emma started to have doubts about following the witch. She was getting farther and farther from home.

When they reached a graveyard, the witch jumped out from behind a tombstone. "Boo!" Then the witch ran away.

Emma ran after her, then hid behind a rock. "Why did you bring me here?" She wasn't afraid anymore, but very much wanted to go home. This was the witch's home, not Emma's.

"I saw that you were alone. I'm alone and need a friend. I showed you all the wonders of my land. Now you have to stay here with me. Only a naughty little unicorn wanders off by itself," the witch said.

Emma started to cry. "I don't want to stay here. I want to go home and clean my room." She promised that she would never wander off again.

"Very well," the witch said. "Have a drink of juice before you go. If you give me your tutu, I will show you the way."

Emma happily handed over the tutu and the witch kept her promise of showing her the way home.

Emma's friends the butterflies welcomed her home.

"Your mother is very worried," they said. "She will be happy to see you."

Emma ran the rest of the way home and
cleaned her room.